Special thanks to
Emily Sharratt

Reading Consultant: Prue Goodwin, lecturer in literacy and children's books.

ORCHARD BOOKS

First published in 2017 by The Watts Publishing Group

1 3 5 7 9 10 8 6 4 2

A CIP catalogue record for this book is available from the British Library.

ISBN 978 1 40835 227 4

Printed and bound in China

The paper and board used in this book are made from wood from responsible sources.

Orchard Books
An imprint of Hachette Children's Group
Part of The Watts Publishing Group Limited
Carmelite House, 50 Victoria Embankment, London EC4Y 0DZ

An Hachette UK Company
www.hachette.co.uk
www.hachettechildrens.co.uk

ALOLA
ADVENTURE

ORCHARD

MEET ASH AND PIKACHU!

ASH

A Pokémon dreamer who wants to have it all – including becoming a Pokémon Master!

PIKACHU

Ash's First Partner Pokémon and long-time companion!

LOOK OUT FOR
THESE POKÉMON

BEWEAR

CHARIZARD

ZUBAT

SALANDIT

YUNGOOS

CONTENTS

PART ONE: HOLIDAY IN ALOLA

PART TWO: THE POKÉMON SCHOOL

PART THREE: NEW LESSONS

PART ONE
Holiday in Alola

CHAPTER ONE

A Special Delivery

Ash and Pikachu were on holiday on Melemele Island in the Alola region. They were having the best time!

"Did you enjoy your Pokémon jet skiing today, Ash?" asked his mother. She and

Mr. Mime had been reading
under a parasol while Ash and
Pikachu played.

"It was so much fun!"
Ash replied happily. "I saw
lots of Pokémon that I've
never seen before."

"That's great," Ash's mother said. "But now you, Mimey and I must get going. We have to take this Pokémon Egg to Professor Oak's cousin." Professor Oak was a friend of theirs from the Kanto region.

"I wonder what kind of Pokémon it is," said Ash.

"You'll just have to wait until it hatches to find out," said his mother.

Ash and his mother got a special Pokémon taxi to take them to the Pokémon School, where Professor Oak's cousin was the headteacher.

Along the way, they stopped at a market for Ash's mother to buy some fruit. While she was choosing berries, Ash and Pikachu explored.

Suddenly, a Pokémon burst from the ground!

"Wow!" said Ash, leaning forward to get a better look.

As he got closer, the Pokémon reached out with its pincer and pinched Ash right on the nose.

"Ow!" Ash shouted.

As he rubbed his nose, the Pokémon scurried back underground.

"Let's catch it," Ash said. "Come on, Pikachu!"

CHAPTER TWO

Surprise!

Ash and Pikachu chased the cheeky Pokémon through town and all the way to some woods.

"Hey, slow down!" Ash shouted after it.

Suddenly, a fruit dropped on to Ash's head from above.

He looked up but he couldn't see anything but trees, although he had the strange feeling he was being watched.

"Where are we?" he said.

Just then, a strange cry rang out in the woods.

"That sounds like a Pokémon," Ash said.

From the bushes emerged a large pink and grey Pokémon. Ash had never seen anything like it before. The Pokémon waved in a friendly way.

"Ah, it's so cute," said Ash, walking towards the Pokémon.

Still waving, the Pokémon reached out with one paw and sliced right through the trunk of a tree, sending it crashing towards Ash.

Ash and Pikachu dodged out of the way just in time to avoid being crushed. Then they watched in horror as the huge Pokémon spun through the air, slicing through tree trunk after tree trunk as though they were the stems of flowers.

Then the Pokémon stopped, looked towards them and gave an ear-piercing cry.

Ash and Pikachu turned and ran. The Pokémon stomped behind them, screaming and sending trees falling to the ground as it went.

At last, the Pokémon stopped chasing them, and Ash and Pikachu were able to slow down and catch their breath.

"What was that all about?" Ash asked.

Suddenly a large shape flew overhead. "What's that?" Ash said with a gasp. "Wow, look, it's a Charizard! Quick, Pikachu, let's follow it!"

CHAPTER THREE

New Friends

Ash and Pikachu chased after the Charizard. They emerged through the trees to see a big building, where hundreds of children and Pokémon were training and playing together.

Ash stared in astonishment. "What is this place?"

He saw a girl in a white hat standing with three Pokémon and he started over towards her.

Her eyes widened in alarm as he approached. "Look out!" she cried.

Ash looked up to see three huge Tauros and their riders thundering towards him. They were racing and they were going too fast to stop.

The Tauros were going to trample him!

At the very last moment, the Tauros riders managed to pull their Pokémon to a halt.

"Are you OK?" the girl in the white hat asked Ash.

"I'm so sorry," said one of the Tauros riders, looking worried.

"You came out of the forest so suddenly!"

"I'm fine, don't worry," said Ash with a shaky laugh. "I'm Ash, by the way. I come from Pallet Town in the Kanto region. This is my friend,

Pikachu. It's nice to meet you!"

"I'm Mallow," replied one of the girls. "And this is the Pokémon School! If you like, I can show you around."

"That would be great!" Ash said, with a grin.

PART TWO
The Pokémon School

CHAPTER FOUR

The Grand Tour

"The Pokémon School is a place where Pokémon and children all learn together," said Mallow, leading Ash around the building. She knocked at a door, and it opened to reveal Ash's mother.

"Mum!" exclaimed Ash.

"You finally made it!" his mother replied. "This is Samson Oak, headteacher of the Pokémon School and Professor Oak's cousin."

"Nice to meet you, Ash," said Samson Oak. "Come on in. I was just about to call my cousin and let him know that you've delivered the egg safely."

"Actually, Mr Oak, I was wondering if I could keep showing Ash around the school," said Mallow.

"I'd love to see more of the school!" Ash agreed.

"All right, you two, off you go," Mr Oak agreed with a chuckle.

As Mallow showed Ash around the classrooms a voice

came from behind them.

"You must be Ash." Ash turned to see a young man in sunglasses and a cap walking towards them.

"This is Professor Kukui," said Mallow.

Just then, there was a loud
roaring noise from outside.
Ash ran to the window. He
saw three children in helmets
talking to a boy from the
Pokémon School. Ash realised
he was the one who had been

riding the Charizard earlier.

"What's happening?" Ash asked Mallow.

"Those three are from Team Skull. They're always bullying us into Pokémon battles. It looks as though they're challenging Kiawe right now."

"Three against one? That's not fair," said Ash. "I'm going to help him!"

CHAPTER FIVE

A Big Battle

Ash ran quickly to the front of the school.

"You shouldn't have blocked our path," he heard one of Team Skull saying to the boy called Kiawe. "If you can beat us in a Pokémon battle, we

might let you walk away. But
if we beat you, that Charizard
will belong to us."

Kiawe narrowed his eyes.
Team Skull released Pokémon
from their Poké Balls. Out
came Salandit, Yungoos and
Zubat, snarling threateningly.

"Tell your Charizard to fight!" Team Skull ordered Kiawe.

"Stop!" shouted Ash. "You're cowards to gang up three against one."

"Oh yeah?" one of the boys from Team Skull sneered. "And

what are you going to do about it?"

"I'm going to fight too!" Ash replied.

"I don't need your help," Kiawe said.

"Be careful, Ash," Mallow called. "Those three are dangerous!" But Ash paid no attention.

"Pikachu, are you ready?" Ash asked. "I choose you!"

Pikachu leapt forward, ready to attack.

"Don't get hurt," Kiawe said.

Then he called to one of his
own Pokémon. "Turtonator,
come out!"

Turtonator burst from
Kiawe's Poké Ball.

"So that's a Turtonator!" Ash
said, grinning.

Kiawe nodded.

Team Skull ordered their Pokémon to attack using their special moves.

"Salandit, show them your strength with Venoshock!"

"Yungoos, use Bite!"

"Zubats, use Leech Life!"

CHAPTER SIX

Holy Smoke!

Ash told Pikachu to use his special Quick Attack move. Pikachu moved so fast he looked like a blur. Team Skull's Salandit Pokémon were soon knocked back, sprawling on to the ground.

"That's fast!" Kiawe had to admit.

Next, Turtonator turned his spines towards Team Skull's Yungoos and Zubat. The Yungoos and Zubat flew together towards Turtonator.

When they touched the spines, they exploded in a blaze of fire and smoke. The attacking Pokémon were sent flying backwards.

"That's a great move!" exclaimed Ash.

"Anything that touches Turtonator's spines explodes," Kiawe explained.

Team Skull weren't ready to give up yet. "Salandit, use Flame Burst!" one of the boys called to his Pokémon.

The Salandit sent flames

shooting towards Pikachu.

"Pikachu, dodge and use Thunderbolt!" Ash shouted hurriedly.

Pikachu's Thunderbolt hit the Salandit with a blast of light and smoke, dazing them.

Ash's new friends cheered from the sidelines.

"I'll finish this," said Kiawe.

Before Ash could reply, Kiawe crossed his arms in front of him. Ash noticed he was wearing a

band around one wrist.

Flames seemed to pour from the wristband until they covered Kiawe and Turtonator.

Team Skull watched in horror, taking a few frightened steps backwards.

"Inferno Overdrive!" shouted Kiawe.

PART THREE

New Lessons

CHAPTER SEVEN

A New Move

"Turtonator!" roared Kiawe's Pokémon. Stomping on the ground, it created a huge fireball, which went rolling towards Team Skull's Pokémon, flattening them at once.

The defeated Pokémon lay

stunned on the ground, smoke from the attack billowing around them. Team Skull drew out their Poké Balls, calling their Pokémon back.

"Using that move wasn't fair," they shouted, retreating on their bikes in a cloud of dust. "We won't forget this!"

"What was that move?" Ash asked, still gaping at Kiawe.

"That was a Z-Move," said Professor Kukui.

He and the others drew closer to Ash and Kiawe.

"What's a Z-Move?" Ash asked.

"They're special moves passed down in the Alola region. Alola has four islands, and each of them has its own Guardian Pokémon, with its

own special moves," Professor
Kukui explained.

"Only those who take part
in a ceremony called the Island
Challenge are able to use
Z-Moves," Kiawe said with
a sniff.

Just then, something flew overhead. Again a fruit dropped on to Ash's head as it passed.

This time, Ash looked up in time to see a flapping of yellow wings disappearing from view. "What was that Pokémon?" Ash exclaimed.

CHAPTER EIGHT

Tapu Koko

"What Pokémon?" the others asked.

Ash looked again, but the mysterious Pokémon had vanished.

"Didn't you see it?" Ash said to the others, feeling confused.

"It was yellow, and about this big." He held his arms out to show them. "It had an orange crest on its head."

The others looked shocked.

"That sounds like …" Mallow began.

"Tapu Koko," Kiawe finished, staring at Ash with a strange look in his eyes.

"You saw Tapu Koko?" Mallow asked. "The Guardian of Melemele Island?"

"That was the Guardian Pokémon?" replied Ash.

That evening, Ash was having dinner with his mother in a restaurant. On a stage some local people were performing a special Alola region fire dance, but Ash just couldn't concentrate.

All he could think about was his day at the Pokémon School, the battle with Team Skull and the mysterious Guardian Pokémon, Tapu Koko. Ash wondered if he would ever be able to use Z-Moves like Kiawe.

"Are you OK, Ash?" asked his mother. "You seem distracted."

Before Ash could answer, a strange cry echoed out through the nearby trees.

Ash looked up in time to see the same Pokémon from earlier

flying through the leaves.

"Tapu Koko!" Ash breathed. He and Pikachu leapt up and began to follow the Guardian Pokémon.

"Where are you going?" Ash's mother called behind him, but Ash didn't stop to answer.

CHAPTER NINE

Inspiration

Together, Ash and Pikachu chased Tapu Koko all the way to a tower high in the city.

At last the Pokémon stopped, hovering in front of Ash. Ash panted, out of breath.

"Wow," he said, amazed,

as he gazed at the famous
Guardian Pokémon of
Melemele Island. The air
around it seemed to sparkle.
"Tapu Koko! Why do you
keep appearing to me? Is
there something you want to
tell me?"

The Pokémon held out
a strange wristband, which
floated over to Ash.

"What's that?" Ash asked.
"It looks like what Kiawe was
wearing."

Tapu Koko nodded at Ash.

Ash reached out for the wristband and instantly was dazzled by a bright light. He put the wristband on. Tapu Koko nodded once more, before turning and flying away. Ash stared in wonder after

the Pokémon, and then at
the band on his wrist. Maybe
he would be able to learn
Z-Moves after all.

A few days later, Ash was
speaking to his mother on the
phone. She was back in Pallet
Town, Ash's home.

"Thanks for letting me stay
on in Alola, Mum!" he said
happily.

"That's all right," she replied.
"I like to see you and Pikachu
having a good time."

"Professor Kukui's house is so cool, there's even a Pokémon training room downstairs!" Ash was bouncing up and down with excitement. "And I can't wait to start at the school. I'm going to learn so much here!"

"Speaking of which," his mother said, "hadn't you better get going?"

"You're right!" Ash cried. "I don't want to be late on my first day at Pokémon School!"

The End

DON'T MISS THESE OTHER OFFICIAL POKÉMON BOOKS